Esther
the Kindness
Fairy

To Esther O'Byrne, with love

Special thanks to Rachel Elliot

ISBN 978-1-338-15767-3

10 9 8 7 6 5 4 3 2 1   17 18 19 20 21

Printed in the U.S.A.   40
First edition, July 2017

Esther
the Kindness
Fairy

by Daisy Meadows

SCHOLASTIC INC.

The Fairyland Palace

Stage

Palace Gardens

Rainspell Pa

Tennis Court & Clubhouse

TENNIS

Sunny Days
B & B

Rainspell Beach

The Friendship Fairies like big smiles.
They want to spread good cheer for miles.
Those pests want people to connect,
And treat one another with respect.

I don't agree! I just don't care!
I want them all to feel despair.
And when their charms belong to me,
Each friend will be an enemy!

Contents

The Start of Summer

"It's so amazing to be back on Rainspell Island again—*together*!" said Kirsty Tate, leaning out her window and taking a deep breath of sea air.

Her best friend, Rachel Walker, clapped her hands and bounced up and down on her tiptoes.

"Today is the start of the most amazing summer vacation *ever*," she said. "I'm sure of it!"

They were sharing a room at the Sunny Days Bed & Breakfast on the island where they had first met and become best friends. They were so happy to be there again on vacation together. The girls shared a quick hug before rushing down the narrow stairs to the cozy breakfast room. Their parents were already there, poring over leaflets about activities on the island.

"I'm sure we can find some new things to do," said Mr. Walker, "even though we have visited this island so many times before."

"How about a nice long hike?" suggested Mr. Tate as the girls slipped into their seats and poured some cereal. "It'd be interesting to explore more of the island—we all love seeing its beautiful plants and trees."

Rachel and Kirsty shared a smile. They had an extra-special secret reason why they loved Rainspell Island so much. It was here that they had first become friends with the fairies!

"Hiking would be a great start to the trip," said Mr. Walker. "Let's head out after breakfast, shall we?"

"Here's something interesting," said Mrs. Walker, holding out a bright yellow flyer. "It's called the Summer Friends Camp."

Rachel took the flyer and read out loud. "'A day camp for children staying on the island. Make new friends and join in lots of fun activities.' It sounds awesome!"

As Kirsty and Rachel were looking
at the flyer and chattering about the
activities, the breakfast-room door
opened and Mr. Holliday came in.
He ran the bed and breakfast, and he
glanced at the flyer as he put some toast
down on the table.

"My daughter Ginny's helping
run that camp with her best friend, Jen,"
he said.

Kirsty and Rachel exchanged a
special smile, wondering if Ginny and
Jen's friendship was as strong as theirs.
They knew that they were lucky to have
each other.

"Is it OK if we go to the Summer
Friends Camp instead of going on the
hike?" Kirsty asked. "It sounds like lots
of fun."

"Of course," said Mr. Tate. "We'll see you later. You can tell us all about it!"

"The Summer Friends Camp is held at Rainspell Park," said Mr. Holliday. "I'm sure you'll have a wonderful time."

When they had finished breakfast, the Tates and the Walkers put on their backpacks and hiking boots and set out on their hike. Rachel and Kirsty waved good-bye and then headed off toward Rainspell Park. The bed and breakfast was on a tree-lined road that overlooked the ocean, and as they walked along they saw the ferry heading toward the island.

"Remember when we met on the ferry that first day?" Rachel asked, smiling at her best friend. "That was one of the best days of my life."

"Mine, too," said Kirsty. "Everything

I do is more fun now that I have you to share it with—including our fairy adventures!"

The girls held hands and smiled when they saw that they were both wearing the friendship bracelets that Florence the Friendship Fairy had given them. Rainspell Island was the place where the girls had first made friends with the fairies, so it had a very special place in their hearts.

"I hope we'll meet some more fairies while we're here," said Rachel. "I love making new fairy friends."

"Fingers crossed we'll make some new human friends, too," Kirsty added. "The Summer Friends Camp sounds like such a fun idea."

They reached the entrance to Rainspell Park and walked through the open gates, gazing around at colorful flowerbeds and huge old trees. The wide gravel paths were dotted with benches, and a large fountain was bubbling and splashing beside the bandstand.

"Look," said Rachel, "there's a sign for the camp."

A bright yellow sign pointed them past the fountain and around a bend. They saw a large tepee-style tent in

the middle of the grass.
It was surrounded by
colorful balloons,
and the sign
next to the
tent said,
*Welcome to
the Summer
Friends Camp!*

Still holding hands, Rachel and
Kirsty walked into the tent. It was
cool inside, and decorated with
rainbow-colored silk. A smiling teenage
girl hurried to greet them. She was
wearing a mint-green name tag that
said, *Jen*, decorated with delicate,
dark-gray birds.

"Welcome to our camp," she said.
"Come and join us!"

A Surprise in the Goal

Peering over Jen's shoulder, Rachel and Kirsty could see another teenage girl standing at a craft table with eight other children. Jen led them over to the table and the other teenager smiled at them.

"Hi, girls, it's great to see you here! I'm Ginny. Right now we're all making name tags. It'd be great if everyone could introduce themselves."

The children smiled at Rachel and Kirsty and went around the table introducing themselves. Then two children named Lara and Oscar made space for the girls to join them.

"Have some markers," said Oscar, moving a cup of markers over so they could both share it.

"I have enough stickers for all of us," added Lara, placing her sticker sheet between them all.

"Thanks, that's so kind of you," said Rachel with a smile.

They both took a blank name tag and started the fun of decorating.

"So is this your first time on the island?" Jen asked Rachel.

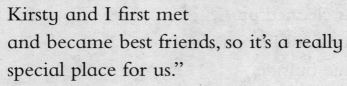

"No, we've been here lots of times," said Rachel. "It's actually where Kirsty and I first met and became best friends, so it's a really special place for us."

"You're so lucky," said Lara as she carefully drew a butterfly on her name tag. "I've been here for three days and I love it. I wish I lived here!"

"It's definitely a great place for friendship," said Ginny, exchanging a smile with Jen.

"Everyone is so nice," Kirsty whispered to Rachel. "I'm really glad we came."

As soon as the name tags were finished and the craft table was cleaned up, Ginny asked everyone to come outside.

"We have two outdoor activities planned for today," she said. "First we'll play a game of soccer, and then Jen and I will challenge you all to a water-balloon fight!"

"Let's split into teams," said Jen. "I can't wait to get started!"

She divided the group into two, and Rachel and Kirsty found themselves on different teams. They grinned at each other—everyone was so friendly that they didn't mind being separated at all!

"All we need now are some goalposts," said Ginny. "Does anyone have anything we can use to mark where the goal is?"

Rachel pulled off her bright pink
hoodie and three of the other children
also donated colorful sweatshirts and
cardigans. Then the positions were
assigned and the game began. Kirsty was
the goalie for her team, and she stood
in the goal with her knees bent and her
heart thumping as Rachel's team brought
the ball closer and closer to her. She felt
nervous because she didn't play soccer

very often and she didn't want to let anyone down.

Lara darted across the field and kicked the ball as hard as she could. The ball flew toward Kirsty, who dived sideways, hands outstretched. She felt it brush her fingertips, but she couldn't quite reach it, and the first goal had been scored.

"GOAL!" yelled Rachel, jumping up and down in delight.

"Good dive, Kirsty!" called Lara.

Kirsty picked herself up and looked around at her team, feeling awful.

"I'm so sorry," she said. "I tried my best."

"Don't worry," said Oscar, jogging over to pat her on the back. "You tried really hard, but that was an amazing goal. Besides, we're just playing for fun. Don't be upset!"

Everyone else on the team was smiling at her, too, and Kirsty felt better right away. The game continued, and soon Oscar had scored a goal for their team. Kirsty started to really enjoy herself.

Rachel was having a good time, too, running up and down the left side of the field and passing to Lara.

When Ginny blew the halftime whistle, the score was 2–2. Rachel jogged over to Kirsty while the others walked across the field to the table of snacks that Jen and Ginny had prepared.

"You've made some amazing saves," said Rachel, hugging her best friend. "You're a really good goalie!"

"Thanks," said Kirsty with a grin. "You and Lara have kept me on my toes!"

"Let's go and get some juice and cookies," said Rachel. "I'm starving!"

As they walked out of the goal area, something caught Kirsty's eye. She looked down and saw that Rachel's hoodie was glowing in a very familiar and magical way.

"Rachel!" Kirsty called in a low voice. "Look!"

They knelt down beside the hoodie, which

was glowing even more brightly. The
girls glanced over at the snack table.
Everyone had their backs to the goal.
Rachel reached out a hand and lifted a
sleeve of the hoodie, and a tiny, chestnut-
haired fairy fluttered out from the folds of
material!

Tea in the Rose Garden

"Hello!" said the fairy in a bubbly voice.
"I'm Esther the Kindness Fairy."

Her pink top was decorated with blue
flowers and her matching skirt flared
out as she gave a happy twirl. She had
a warm, easy smile and her dark eyes
shone with friendliness.

"Hello, Esther," said
Rachel. "It's
great to meet
you."

"We always
love meeting
new fairies,"
added Kirsty
with a smile.

"I've come to invite you to Fairyland
for a tea party with the Friendship
Fairies," said Esther. "We've been wanting
to meet you for a long time—we've
heard so much about you both! Will you
come? You won't miss a moment of the
Summer Friends Camp—time in the
human world will stop while you're in
Fairyland."

Kirsty and Rachel didn't hesitate!

"Yes, please!"
they said
together.

They
glanced
over at
the other
children.
No one was
looking their
way. Esther waved
her wand and a flurry of
golden sparkles surrounded the girls.
They were dazzled, and closed their eyes
as they felt themselves shrinking to fairy
size. Then gossamer wings appeared on
their backs, and a wonderful scent filled
the air. They opened their eyes and
saw that Rainspell Park had vanished.

They were standing in a small Fairyland garden that was filled with roses of every color. In the center of the garden was a white table, upon which was the most wonderful tea party spread that the girls had ever seen. A five-tiered cake stand was filled with meringues, cookies,

macarons, eclairs, and tiny cupcakes in jewel-tone colors. The bottom was filled with bite-size triangular sandwiches, and a rose-patterned teapot steamed merrily beside matching cups and saucers.

"Welcome to our tea party!" said a chorus of tinkling voices. Three other fairies hurried to greet them, their hands outstretched.

"Let me introduce you all," said Esther. "This is Mary the Sharing Fairy, Mimi the Laughter Fairy, and Clare the Caring Fairy—my fellow Friendship Fairies. It's our job to keep all friendships strong and happy."

"What a wonderful job!" said Rachel. "How do you do it?"

"With a little help from our magical objects," said Mimi with a laugh.

Each of the four fairies took out a magical object and laid it on the white table for the girls to see. Rachel and Kirsty were enchanted to see Esther's heart brooch, Mimi's smiley-face pendant, Mary's yin-yang charm, and Clare's mood ring. While they were examining the objects, the fairies poured tea and filled little plates with a selection of dainty sandwiches, mini tea cakes, and mouthwatering appetizers. The girls couldn't resist trying a little of everything! As they sampled the cakes and sipped tea, the fairies showed them all the different roses in the garden. Esther knew the name of each flower. They were sniffing a thornless rose called Titania, named after the queen, when they heard an evil cackle. Everyone jumped and turned

around. To their horror, they saw that
a ring of goblins, holding hands, had
surrounded the little white table. Jack
Frost was standing on top of the table,
and all the delicate cakes and sandwiches
were being trampled under his feet.

"Get down from there right now!" Esther demanded.

She and the other fairies darted forward, but Jack Frost hurled a bolt of blue lightning at them, and they had to dive sideways to avoid it.

Rachel and Kirsty watched helplessly as Jack Frost scooped up the fairies' magical objects and tossed them to the goblins one by one.

30

"Take these to the human world and find some friends for me," he barked at them. "I want to be super-powerful, so I need lots of friends to boss around, not just you miserable fools!"

"No!" cried the girls together.

But Jack Frost and the goblins disappeared with a deafening clap of icy magic.

The fairies joined the girls, their smiles gone.

"That awful Jack Frost!" cried Rachel. "Why does he have to do such horrible things? Why can't he just go and make friends himself, without stealing things that belong to other people?"

"He doesn't understand what friendship is," said Esther in a sad voice. "He's never been able to recognize true friendship—and now that he and his goblins have our magical objects, nobody else will have true friendship, either."

"Then we have to get your objects back quickly," said Kirsty. "Let's hurry before Jack Frost ruins all friendships forever!"

"What about *our* friendship?" asked Rachel in a quiet, worried voice. "Will we start arguing when we get back to the human world?"

Esther frowned, deep in thought. Then her gaze fell on the friendship bracelets that the girls were wearing.

"I have an idea," she said.

She held up her wand and it started to glow. Then she spoke, and her voice sounded as if it were echoing around all of Fairyland.

"Florence, we need you! Our plans
have gone wrong.
We're in the rose garden—please
don't be long!"

Unkind Words

A few seconds later, Florence flew into the garden and landed beside the other fairies. They gasped out the story of what had happened, and she looked alarmed.

"Jack Frost must be stopped," she exclaimed, shaking back her blond hair.

"Can you help to protect the girls' friendship so that they can try to get our magical objects back?" Esther asked.

Florence nodded, and asked the girls to hold up their bracelets. She pointed her wand at them and closed her eyes, and a thin spiral of rainbow-colored fairy dust coiled out of her wand and wrapped around the girls' wrists in a figure eight. The bracelets glowed for a moment and then Florence opened her eyes.

"I've used my 'Friends through Thick

and Thin' spell on your bracelets," she explained. "It means that your friendship won't be affected by the loss of the magical objects, but the spell will only last for a few days. You have to find the objects soon!"

"We will," Rachel promised. "Thank you, Florence."

They hugged their fairy friends good-bye, and then Esther held their hands and whisked them back to the human world. Once again, they were kneeling down beside Rachel's pink hoodie. As usual, no time had passed while they had been gone, and the other children were still at the snack table. But there was no laughter or happy chatter. Instead, all Rachel and Kirsty could hear was arguing.

"Lara, you took my cookie!" Oscar was yelling. "Give it back!"

"This is your fault," Jen grumbled to Ginny. "Why didn't you buy more cookies?"

"Why didn't *you* buy any orange juice?" Ginny retorted. "It's ridiculous to only have apple juice!"

The other children were squabbling, too,
and Rachel and Kirsty listened in dismay
as the arguments got
worse. Eventually
they saw Ginny
hold up the
palm of her
hand to Jen's
face.

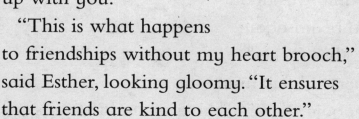

"Don't even
talk to me
anymore," she
snapped. "I'm fed
up with you."

"This is what happens
to friendships without my heart brooch,"
said Esther, looking gloomy. "It ensures
that friends are kind to each other."

Kirsty's eyes filled with tears. "Everyone

is being mean, and it's all Jack Frost's fault," she said. "We have to get the Friendship Fairies' magical objects back before these friendships are ruined forever."

"We will," said Rachel, giving her best friend a hug.

Like Kirsty, she was scared that they might lose their friendship if Jack Frost could not be stopped.

Just then, the other children started walking back toward them. Halftime was over, and the game was about to begin again. Esther tucked herself back inside the hoodie marking the goal and the girls joined their teams.

Suddenly, a new boy in a bright green soccer uniform ran onto the field. The other children ran over and gathered around him.

"Join our team!" called Lara.

"No, our team!" Oscar yelled. "Ignore her!"

The boy joined Lara's team, and the game began. This time, it wasn't as much fun. There were a lot of tackles, and there was even some cheating.

Ginny and Jen kept disagreeing about how to referee the match, and it seemed to drag on forever. Then Lara got the ball and began to dribble it toward the goal.

"To me, Lara!" Rachel called. "I'm free!"

But Lara just scowled at her and passed the ball to the new boy instead. The other children immediately moved out of his way—even the opposing team! He had a clear path down the field toward Kirsty's goal, and she got ready to stop him from scoring. He took a shot and the ball hurtled toward her. She jumped up and caught it . . . then let it go and made sure that it rolled between the goalposts.

"GOAL!" shouted the new boy, and Jen blew the whistle to show that it was the end of the game.

The new boy's team cheered wildly as he pulled the hem of his shirt over his head and ran around in circles. Rachel sprinted over to Kirsty.

"You dropped the ball on purpose," she said. "Why?"

Kirsty shrugged, feeling helpless.

"I have no idea," she said. "I couldn't seem to stop myself."

They looked over to where the new boy was now doing a handstand in celebration. His feet waved in the air.

"Look how big his feet are," said Kirsty.

"They're really, *really* big," Rachel agreed.

Then they both had the same thought at exactly the same moment.

"He's a goblin!"

Esther's Brooch

Esther had heard every word, and she couldn't bear to stay hidden for a moment longer. She fluttered up from the hoodie marking the goal.

"I had to come look," she said, tucking herself under Kirsty's hair. "Where's the goblin?"

Rachel pointed to where the other children were lifting the goblin up on their shoulders, pushing and shoving one another out of the way at the same time.

Esther drew in her breath in shocked surprise.

"Look at his shirt!" she exclaimed.

"He's wearing a brooch," said Kirsty.

"I'm sure you're not supposed to wear jewelery during a game."

"Forget about the rules," said Rachel. "Look at the brooch!"

Kirsty narrowed her eyes and squinted, then gasped.

"It's the magical heart brooch!" she cried. "No wonder everyone is being so nice to him, and not to anyone else!"

"We'll never get it back now," said Esther, looking miserable.

"Of course we will," said Rachel in her most encouraging voice. "We've found it, so we're a huge step closer to getting it back. All we have to do is figure out a plan."

Kirsty was still watching the goblin, who was bragging gleefully about his amazing goal.

"He thinks he's really good at soccer," she said. "That gives me an idea. Esther, could you use your magic to make a soccer shirt that the goblin will think is really amazing?"

As quick as a wink, Esther waved her wand and a bright green soccer shirt was hanging in the air in front of Kirsty. There was a sparkly green star on the back, behind the words, "Soccer Star." Then the shirt gave a little wriggle, folded itself neatly, and landed in Kirsty's outstretched arms.

"Time for a swap!" said Kirsty, smiling.

She and Rachel hurried over to join the crowd of children. They squeezed through the huddle until they reached the goblin, who was now down on the ground again.

"That was an amazing goal," said Rachel. "Truly incredible."

"I know," said the goblin, blowing on his fingernails and polishing them on his shirt.

"We have this shirt for you, so everyone can see what a star you are," said Kirsty, showing him the new green shirt.

"Wow, it's perfect for me!" exclaimed the goblin, his eyes widening. "Give it to me."

"We can only let you have it as a trade," said Rachel. "If you'll let us have your shirt as a souvenir, we'll give you this one. There isn't another one like it in the whole world."

The goblin gazed longingly at the star shirt, but then he shook his head.

"I don't want to trade," he said.

"Oh!" said Rachel. "But—"

"Get out of his way," said Oscar, pushing the girls aside. "You're crowding him!"

The girls would have tried to persuade the goblin again, but at that moment Ginny called to them from the tent.

"Time for the water-balloon fight! Come and get your balloons!" She held up a bag of balloons.

Jen snatched the bag and went to fill them with water from a tap near the fountain.

The children ran over to watch as
she made a big pile of colorful water
balloons. Rachel and Kirsty followed,
Kirsty tucking the shirt into her pocket as
she went.

"Hurry up, Jen," said Ginny. "You're too
slow."

"I'm faster than *you* would be," Jen
retorted.

When the pile was finished, everyone
surged forward, jabbing one another
with their elbows and trying to get to
the balloons first. Rachel and Kirsty
stood back and waited their turn. But
when their turn came, all the balloons
were gone. They looked at Ginny, who
shrugged.

"Tough luck," she said. "You should have
pushed your way in, like everyone else."

"We really have to get that brooch back," Rachel muttered. "Everyone is being so mean!"

The water-balloon fight was already in full swing and the goblin was throwing a lot of balloons, cackling as the children got wetter and wetter. But no one was throwing any balloons at him.

"The brooch is making everyone want to be nice to him," said Esther, peeking out from under Kirsty's hair.

The goblin seemed delighted that he wasn't getting wet.

"I'm the best and you're the worst!" he jeered at the other children, blowing loud raspberries and dancing around in front of them. "I'm the only one who isn't wet! I'm the quickest! I'm the greatest!"

He shrieked with laughter and hopped over to the fountain, hurling balloon after balloon at the children.

"He doesn't want to get wet," said Rachel, and a little idea popped into her mind. "If we can soak him, maybe he'll take the shirt off to get dry."

"But how can we get him wet?" asked Kirsty. "We don't have a single water balloon."

"Who needs a water balloon?" asked Rachel with a grin. "He's standing right next to the fountain!"

Forgiving Friends

The girls ducked out of sight behind
the Friends Camp tent and, with a flick
of her wand, Esther turned them both
into fairies. They flew over the heads of
the other children, who were still busy
throwing water balloons at one another.
The goblin saw the fairies speeding
toward him and scowled.

"Leave me alone!" he squawked, jumping up onto the side of the fountain and flinging water balloons at them. "I know what you want, and you're not getting it!"

"The brooch doesn't belong to you!" cried Kirsty, dodging a red water balloon.

"Who cares about that?" the goblin shouted. "I love it! It makes everyone want to be my friend. Besides, I need it to bring some friends back to the Ice Castle for Jack Frost."

He had run out of water balloons now, but the fairies kept flying around his head as they replied.

"If you're kind to people, they'll want to be your friend anyway," said Esther.

"You should tell that to Jack Frost," added Rachel.

They whizzed
around the goblin
faster and faster,
and he started
to wobble.
Then he lost
his balance
and *SPLASH!*
He fell into the
fountain.

"Wahhh!" he
wailed, pulling himself out and falling
onto the grass with a squelch. "I'm
soaking wet!"

Kirsty whispered to Esther, who waved
her wand again and returned the girls
to human size. Kirsty pulled the Soccer
Star shirt from her pocket, while
Rachel held out a big, fluffy towel. She

wrapped it around the goblin's shoulders as he was wringing out his shirt, and he pulled it closer around himself.

"We could still give you this nice, dry Soccer Star shirt in exchange for Esther's magical brooch," said Kirsty.

The wet goblin looked up at her, shivering with cold. He gazed at the dry shirt with the sparkly star.

"Do you really think I can make friends without the magical brooch?" he asked in a small voice.

"Of course you can!" said Rachel.

"No problem!" said Kirsty.

Esther nodded, and the goblin took a deep breath.

"All right," he said.

He pulled off the wet shirt and held it out to Esther. As soon as she touched the brooch, it shrank to fairy size. The goblin pulled on the dry shirt and grinned.

"Thank you both for your help," said Esther, fluttering over to hover in front of Rachel and Kirsty. "I can't wait to tell the other Friendship Fairies that one of our magical objects is back where it belongs."

"I hope we'll see you again soon," said Rachel.

Esther blew them a kiss, waved, and then disappeared back to Fairyland, leaving a golden shimmer in the air.

Just then, the other children turned and waved to Rachel and Kirsty. The goblin hid behind Rachel's back.

"Come on," said Rachel in a kind voice. "Come and join in."

The goblin was very shy at first, but all the other children were being kind again, and they welcomed him with big smiles.

"Sorry you didn't get to join in the water-balloon fight," said Oscar. "I'm afraid we've used up all the balloons."

"Never mind," said Kirsty. "We can help you clean up!"

Ginny and Jen made a game out of cleaning up, and it wasn't long before every single burst balloon had been picked up. The goblin held the trash bag while the other children put the balloon pieces into it.

"Thank you," said Lara, and the goblin gave her a wide grin.

"You're doing a great job," Ginny added, patting his bony head.

Jen slipped her arm through Ginny's and leaned closer.

"I'm sorry for being so grumpy earlier," she whispered.

"Me, too," Ginny replied. "I can't think why I was so unkind."

Kirsty and Rachel exchanged a smile when they heard this. They knew why kindness had disappeared for a while— and they were delighted to see that it had returned now that Esther had her brooch back.

When the Summer Friends Camp finished for the day, the goblin scampered off to the Ice Castle. Kirsty and Rachel waved good-bye to Lara, Oscar, and the others. They walked back to the Sunny Days Bed & Breakfast, and saw their parents coming back from their hike in the opposite direction.

"Did you have a good time?" asked Mrs. Walker, hugging them.

"It was tons of fun," said Kirsty.

"We made some great new friends," Rachel added. "Can we go back again tomorrow?"

Their parents agreed, and the girls shared a secret smile.

"I'm looking forward to more adventures with our fairy friends, too," Kirsty whispered.

"Oh, Kirsty," said Rachel, her eyes sparkling. "That goes without saying!"

RAINBOW magic™

THE Friendship FAIRIES

Rachel and Kirsty found Esther's
missing magic brooch. Now it's
time for them to help

Mary

the Sharing Fairy!

Join their next adventure in this
special sneak peek . . .

Painting Plans

"I can't wait to find out what we'll be doing at the Summer Friends Camp today," said Kirsty Tate.

She grinned at her best friend, Rachel Walker, who was bouncing up and down on a hoppity hop. They were inside a brightly colored tent in Rainspell Park, where the vacation day camp was based.

"Whatever it is, I'm sure it'll be fun," said Rachel, her blond curls flying around her head as she bounced. "We'll be together!"

Rachel and Kirsty had been friends ever since their first meeting on Rainspell Island. It was an extra-special place for them because they had also become friends with the fairies during that first visit.

This time they were staying at the Sunny Days Bed & Breakfast with their parents. They had attended the Summer Friends Camp on their first day, and were excited to learn that the teenage girls who ran it, Ginny and Jen, were also best friends. Today was their second day of vacation, and they were both looking forward to finding out what Ginny and Jen had planned.

The tent was already ringing with laughter. Oscar and Lara, who they had met the previous day, were practicing one-handed cartwheels. When they collapsed to the ground, out of breath and giggling, Rachel and Kirsty came over to join them.

"Good morning!" said Lara in a cheerful voice. "It's great to see you here again. We're really looking forward to today."

"We are, too," said Kirsty. "We were just wondering what we'll be doing."

"Wonder no more!" said Ginny's friendly voice behind them. "We have something really awesome planned for today."

The children looked around and saw Ginny and Jen standing in the tent entrance, arm in arm. Several other children crowded around them.

"We're going to paint a mural on the tennis clubhouse," said Jen, giving a little hop of excitement. "I'm so thrilled that we have the chance to do this. I know you're all super-creative, and we're going to make the best mural ever."

Chattering and giggling, Rachel and Kirsty headed across the park with the others. The clubhouse stood at the entrance to the tennis courts, and Jen and Ginny led everyone around to the back. They saw a small picnic area on a wooden deck, and Jen pointed at the long side wall of the clubhouse.

"This is the wall we're going to paint," she said. "They want us to brighten up the picnic area."

"What are we going to paint?" asked Oscar.

"The theme of the mural is friendship," said Ginny. "We thought that we could start by painting the word *friendship* on the wall. Then we can decorate it."

Jen took out a big book filled with letters and patterns.

RAINBOW magic

Which Magical Fairies Have You Met?

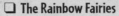

- ❑ The Rainbow Fairies
- ❑ The Weather Fairies
- ❑ The Jewel Fairies
- ❑ The Pet Fairies
- ❑ The Sports Fairies
- ❑ The Ocean Fairies
- ❑ The Princess Fairies
- ❑ The Superstar Fairies
- ❑ The Fashion Fairies
- ❑ The Sugar & Spice Fairies
- ❑ The Earth Fairies
- ❑ The Magical Crafts Fairies
- ❑ The Baby Animal Rescue Fairies
- ❑ The Fairy Tale Fairies
- ❑ The School Day Fairies
- ❑ The Storybook Fairies
- ❑ The Friendship Fairies

 SCHOLASTIC

Find all of your favorite fairy friends at
scholastic.com/rainbowmagic

HiT entertainment

RMFAIRY17